written by
Emma Otheguy

illustrated by
Ana Ramírez González

A SLED FOR GABO

atheneum

Atheneum Books for Young Readers • New York London Toronto Sydney New Delhi

The day it snowed
Gabo followed the whistling sound
of an old steam radiator
into the kitchen.

He stood on tiptoe
and glimpsed a metal can
bobbing and bouncing in the water.
Yum, he thought
before Mami came
and shooed Gabo away.

Gabo pressed his face to the window,
and his warm breath bloomed a cloud of fog
onto the glass.

He wiped it off and saw
kids from his new school
tugging sleds up the hill,
then coasting down,
whooping
and shrieking all the while.

Gabo didn't have a sled.
His socks were cotton, not wool.
He didn't have waterproof boots.

He did have a hat with a pom-pom,
but that was much too small.

"Vamos a resolver," Mami said.
They were going to figure it out.

One sock, two socks, three socks, four.
Gabo's feet were toasty warm.
Papi's hat slipped over his eyes,
and Gabo rolled up the brim.

Plastic bags are waterproof,
so Mami tied them to Gabo's sneakers.

Mami opened the door
and they looked at the houses,
all in a row.
Against the slate-gray sky
the colors popped.

"Maybe I should go and find a sled," said Gabo, and with a little push from Mami, he did.

¡RINNN! ¡RINNN!
¡GUAU! ¡GUAU!

Señor Ramos's dog, Sancho,
barked joyfully
to see Gabo at the door.

"Señor Ramos, do you have a sled?" Gabo asked.

"I don't have a sled," Señor Ramos said.
"But I am making guava jam on toast for Isa,
my granddaughter who is coming to visit.
Isa is just your age. Why don't you stay a while?"

"No gracias," said Gabo,
who was much too shy
for anyone just his age.

Outside, Gabo played with Misifú,
a cat who lived on the cover
of a manhole and belonged to nobody
and everyone at once.

Misifú puffed his chest,
and so did Gabo.

Misifú shook out his coat,
and so did Gabo,
scattering icy snow.

"Gabo, mi amor!"

"Hola, Señora Tobón," said Gabo.

"What are you doing with Misifú,
    instead of playing on the hill?"

"I don't have a sled," Gabo explained.

Señora Tobón shook her head.
"You don't need a sled to play.
¡Mira! My mango is ripe and ready to share."

She held out the mango, carefully cubed,
and nodded toward the snowy slope
where schoolkids were skidding, gliding,
and bumping down the hill.

Gabo reached into his pocket
and felt his leftover Christmas turrón.
There were two crunchy candy pieces:
One could be for Gabo,
and one for a new friend,
but Gabo was much too shy
to hand out mango cubes
and leftover Christmas turrón.

Gabo dragged his feet.
The plastic bags started to slip.
The snow was turning gray
from all the traffic of the town.

A lady in the distance
waved a yellow-mittened hand.

"Tío Tim!" Gabo yelled. "Madrina!"

Tío Tim scooped Gabo into the air.
He almost skimmed the sky.

And what was that?
Behind Madrina's back
there was a . . .

"Oh," said Gabo,
feeling very small
and very sad.

The plastic tray
was from the school cafeteria
where Madrina worked.
It was wrapped with a bow.

But the plastic tray
was not a sled.

"Sancho!" yelled a girl
who could only be Isa,
Señor Ramos's granddaughter.

Sancho bounded toward Gabo
and leaped into his arms.

Sancho was perfectly happy,
and Gabo forgot to be shy.

"Could I have a turn on your sled?" Isa asked.

"I don't have a sled," Gabo said sadly.

"Of course you do!"
And on the plastic tray,
Isa swooped right down
to the bottom of the hill.

She ran back up,
and on that tray . . .

Gabo coasted down,
whooping
and shrieking all the while.

When the snowy day
turned to icy dusk
and the sledding hill was empty,
the old steam radiator whistled
and the metal can
sat on the counter to cool.

Gabo handed out spoons,
and Papi turned the crank
of the can opener.

"DULCE DE LECHE!"
yelled Gabo and Isa
at the exact same time,
then dipped their spoons into the can.

Gabo licked his lips
and reached into his pocket,
where there was one more treat
that Gabo was *not* too shy to share.